THIS IS THE
FEAST

To Larry and Marie Shore, a grand *thank you*
for all your help and encouragement
—D.Z.S.

To my parents with love and thanks beyond measure
—M.L.

I would like to acknowledge and give a very special thanks to editor
Ellen Stein for her excellent guidance and direction on this book,
and above all for taking a chance on a new writer.
—D.Z.S.

HISTORICAL NOTE

In 1620 a group of 102 men, women, and children sailed on the *Mayflower* to America, to establish a settlement where they could find religious freedom. Two months later the Pilgrims, or First Comers, sighted land. After weeks of scouting, they settled in a deserted Patuxet village in what is now Massachusetts, next to fields already cleared by these Indians, who had been struck with disease. They named their new home Plymouth.

The Pilgrims befriended Squanto, the only surviving member of the Patuxet Indian tribe. He taught the Pilgrims how to fish, hunt, and plant corn they had found. Without his help, the Pilgrims might not have survived.

The harvest of 1621 was plentiful. Governor William Bradford invited Squanto and neighboring Indians to join in a three-day celebration: the first Thanksgiving.

THIS IS THE FEAST Text copyright © 2008 by Diane Z. Shore Illustrations copyright © 2008 by Megan Lloyd-Thompson Manufactured in China. All rights reserved. No part of this book may be used or reproduced in any manner whatsoever without written permission except in the case of brief quotations embodied in critical articles and reviews. For information address HarperCollins Children's Books, a division of HarperCollins Publishers, 1350 Avenue of the Americas, New York, NY 10019. www.harpercollinschildrens.com
Library of Congress Cataloging-in-Publication Data   Shore, Diane ZuHone.   This is the feast / by Diane Z. Shore ; illustrated by Megan Lloyd. — 1st ed.   p.   cm.   ISBN 978-0-06-623794-7 (trade bdg.) — ISBN 978-0-06-623795-4 (lib. bdg.)   1. Thanksgiving Day—Juvenile poetry. 2. Pilgrims (New Plymouth Colony)—Juvenile poetry. 3. Wampanoag Indians—Juvenile poetry. 4. Indians of North America—Juvenile poetry. 5. Children's poetry, American. I. Lloyd, Megan, ill. II. Title.   PS3619.H665T5 2008   2007025795   811'.6 dc22   CIP   AC
Designed by Stephanie Bart-Horvath 1 2 3 4 5 6 7 8 9 10 ❖ First Edition

THIS IS THE
FEAST

by Diane Z. Shore
illustrated by Megan Lloyd

HarperCollins *Publishers*

This is the Mayflower, sturdy and strong.
Her sails skim the skies as she journeys along.

These are the Pilgrims, down on their knees,
seasick and frightened on rough, rolling seas.

These are the storms and the battering gales,
crashing the decks and thrashing the sails.

Land ho! America! World unknown,
a wilderness wild, a place to call home
that greeted the Pilgrims, fearful but brave,
who sailed off to freedom through wind and through wave
across the Atlantic, so far and so wide.
"Thanks be to God, our strength and our guide."

These are the oak trees, bundled in snow,
felled for the houses as bitter winds blow.

This is the hearth, soothing the soul,
as death and disease take a terrible toll.

This is the corn, a treasure of maize,
black, yellow, red, and blue nuggets ablaze.

These are the fields, stubbled, unclaimed,
cleared by Patuxets before the plague came,
and found by the Pilgrims exploring ashore
far from the baskets of nuggets galore
that colored the gray, weary days of despair.
"Thanks be to God for the lives He has spared."

These are the birch trees, budding in spring,
nestlings of robins and promise they bring.

These are the Indians, fearful, aware—
"Welcome" their greeting, approaching with care.

This is the corn seed, planted in mounds
with herring to nourish the seed in the ground.

This is Tisquantum, or Squanto his name,
a keen-eyed Patuxet the plague didn't claim,
who helped sow the corn, the colorful maize,
and shared with the Pilgrims his knowledge and ways
of fishing and trapping and hunting the land.
"Thanks be to God for this wise, clever man."

These are the elm trees, brushing the skies
as summer days dawn and Pilgrims arise.

This is the shallop, skimming the tide,
flashing with cod to be salted and dried.

These are the corn shoots, fountains of maize,
weeded and tilled through hot, sunny days.

These are the gardens, leafy and green,
crowded with cucumber, spinach, and bean
that sprouted near cornfields, threaded with vines
of blossoming pumpkins and squash of all kinds
that flowered the Cape that was nurtured by hand.
"Thanks be to God for this bountiful land."

These are the maples, in forests ablaze,
where wild turkeys run and golden deer graze.

These are the plums and cranberries tart,
picked and preserved with gladdening heart.

These are the cornstalks, soldiers of maize,
gathered in sheaves during harvesting days.

These are the baskets of plentiful crops,
spilling with tassels and vegetable tops
and brimming with berries and chestnuts and plums
that ripened in forests where golden deer run—
a harvest of plenty, all gathered with pride.
"Thanks be to God, who doth us provide!"

This is the Feast the Pilgrims prepared
and welcomed the neighboring Indians, who shared
in the singing and dancing, a joyous three days
of heartily feasting on mountains of maize
and puddings and codfish and lobsters and meat
of the deer and wild fowl, all roasted and sweet,
and spread on a table of long wooden planks,
then blessed with a prayer of heartwarming thanks
for the friendships and harvest and bountiful land
that was seeded and weeded and reaped by the hands
of our hardworking forefathers, daring and brave,
seeking freedom of worship through wind and through wave,
as they sailed on the *Mayflower*, plodding but strong,
her sails filled with dreams as she journeyed along.

This is Thanksgiving, a time to remember
the friendships and freedoms we all share together.